Bed, Bats, & Beyond

BY JOAN HOLUB
ILLUSTRATED BY MERNIE GALLAGHER-COLE

For Paul, my favorite brother.
—J.H.

Text copyright © 2008 Joan Holub

Illustrations copyright © 2008 Mernie Gallagher-Cole

Cataloging-in-Publication

Holub, Joan.
Bed, Bats, & Beyond / by Joan Holub ; illustrated by Mernie Gallagher-Cole.
        p. ; cm.
ISBN 978-1-58196-077-8
Ages 7 and up.—Summary: It's dawn and time for bats to go to bed, but Fang's brother Fink
can't sleep. Soon the whole family tries different bedtime stories to lull Fink to sleep.
1. Bats—Juvenile fiction. 2. Bedtime—Juvenile fiction. [1. Bats—Fiction. 2. Bedtime—Fiction.]
I. Title. II. Author. III. Ill.
PZ7.H7427 Bed 2008
[Fic] dc22
OCLC: 209959824

Published by Darby Creek Publishing
7858 Industrial Parkway
Plain City, OH 43064
www.darbycreekpublishing.com

Printed in the United States of America

2 4 6 8 10 9 7 5 3 1

Contents

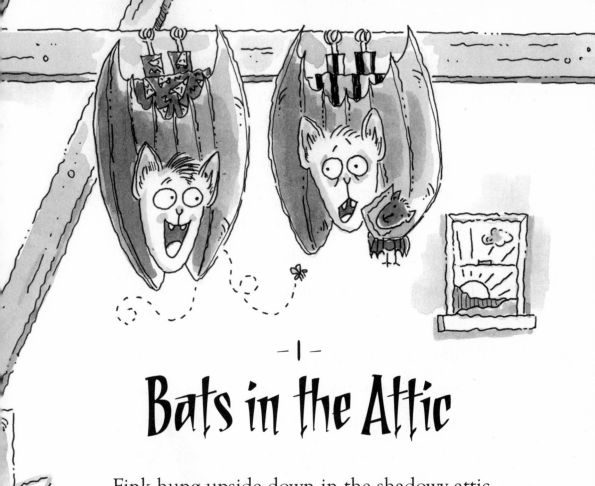

— 1 —
Bats in the Attic

Fink hung upside down in the shadowy attic. Outside, the sun was coming up. It was time for bats to go to bed. But he couldn't sleep.

So he elbowed his brother Fang—hard.

Fang opened his eyes. "Huh?"

"I can't sleep," said Fink.

Fang yawned and scratched his belly. "Why not? Are you afraid the Swamp Owl will get you? *Whooo!*"

"What Swamp Owl?" squeaked Fink.

Fang laughed. His long, white teeth glowed in the dark. "Just kidding," he said. "Did you try counting mosquitoes? That's supposed to help you sleep."

"Yes. It didn't work," said Fink.

"Did you try counting spiders?"

Fink nodded. "Didn't work."

"Did you try—" Fang began.

"Forget it! Counting stuff doesn't work," said Fink.

"Okay, okay. Calm down. And don't worry," said Fang. His eyes glittered as he leaned closer. "Because I know something that'll put you right to sleep. A scary story."

"Really?" asked Fink, looking unsure.

Fang nodded. "A scary story is just the right thing for a sunny morning. And I know the perfect one. Here goes . . ."

SWAMP OWL:
A SCARY STORY

Once there was a scary, stinky swamp with purple fog and green gloom all around it. And in that scary, stinky swamp lived something very scary and stinky. A monster. And its name was . . . Swamp Owl.

Swamp Owl spent every night making up
monstrous recipes in his swampy, stinky
kitchen. Every recipe included bats. And as he
wrote his recipes, he burped out a song:

Bats with ice cream.

Bats with tea.

Bats with frosting.

Bats for me!

Bats with sprinkles.

Bats on toast.

Bats are what

I love the most!

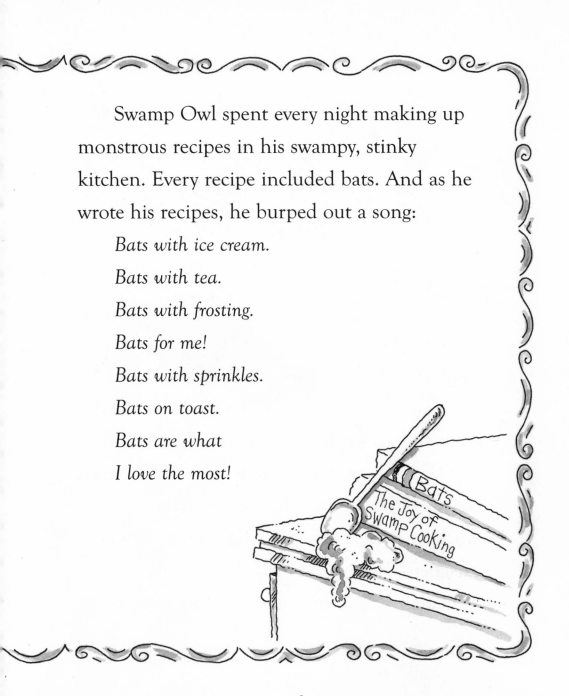

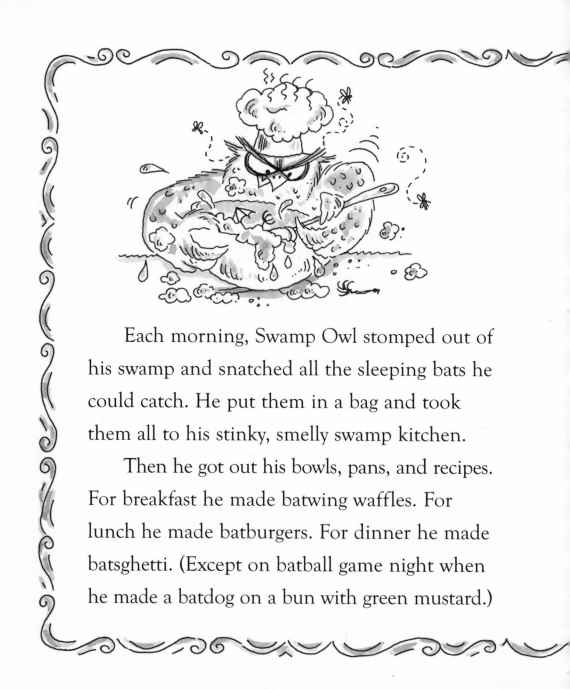

Each morning, Swamp Owl stomped out of his swamp and snatched all the sleeping bats he could catch. He put them in a bag and took them all to his stinky, smelly swamp kitchen.

Then he got out his bowls, pans, and recipes. For breakfast he made batwing waffles. For lunch he made batburgers. For dinner he made batsghetti. (Except on batball game night when he made a batdog on a bun with green mustard.)

One day, it was Swamp Owl's one-hundredth birthday.

I need something special to celebrate, he thought. So he got out his recipes. *If I had two tasty bats, I could bake this batberry cake,* he decided.

So he stomped off to find two tasty bats. Along the way, he burped this song:

Batty cakes!
Batty cakes!
Two bats
are all it takes.

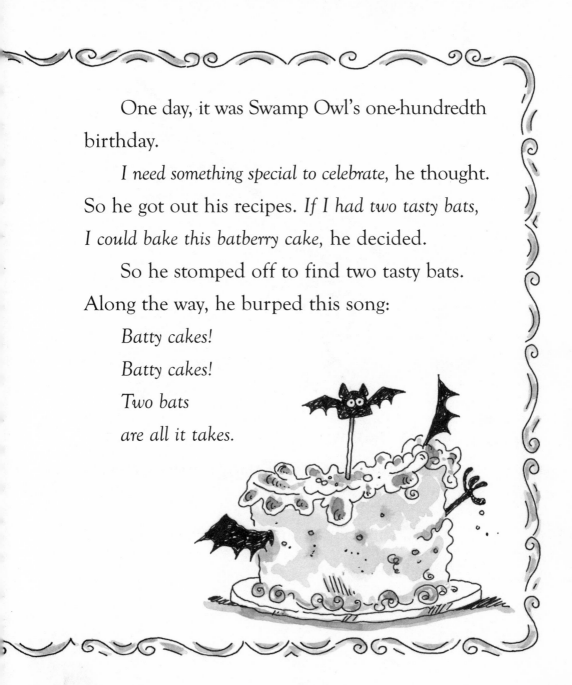

He saw skinny bats in caves and fat bats in
trees, but none were quite right for his recipe.
So he kept looking.

Then, through an attic window, he saw two
brother bats.

Perfect! he thought.

"Hey there, bat boys! Do you want to come to my birthday party?" he called to them, waking them up.

"Maybe. What kind of cake are you having?" asked the bat brothers. They swooped out the window to hear more.

Swamp Owl grinned. "Bat cake! Ha! Ha! Ha!" With that, he grabbed them and stuffed them both into his grocery sack.

Then he headed home.

Inside the sack, the two bats were scared. But they were smart, too, and quickly hatched a plan.

"We're magic birthday bats," they told him from inside the dark sack. "If you let us go, we'll grant you a birthday wish."

"Oh goody!" said Swamp Owl. He opened the sack and looked at them. "I wish . . ."

"Close your eyes first," warned the bat brothers, "or your wish won't come true."

"But if I do that, you'll fly away," said Swamp Owl.

"No, we won't," the bats fibbed.

"Okay, then," said Swamp Owl.

He stared at the bats and licked his chops. Then he closed his eyes and made a wish.

"I wish that instead of waiting . . . ,"
Swamp Owl began.

The bats got ready to fly.

". . . I could gobble you both up right now!"
Swamp Owl finished.

And just as the bats zoomed out of the
sack, Swamp Owl grabbed them and gobbled
them up, singing . . .

Batty cakes!
Batty cakes!
Two bites
are all it takes.
Burp!

 **THE END**

Fang looked at Fink. Fink's eyes were shut tight. His teeth were chattering.

"Are you asleep?" Fang whispered.

Fink's eyes popped open. He frowned at Fang. "No way! I'm too worried about owl monsters now. Thanks a lot."

— 2 —

Bossy, Bossy

Just then, their big brother Batrick flew out of his room in the chimney. He did a cool loop-the-loop around the umbrella.

Next, he did a corkscrew through the lampshade. Then he did a tuck-and-roll over the table.

"I'm the boss while Mom's out," said Batrick. "And I say cut the bat chat and go to bed."

"But Fink can't sleep," explained Fang. "I told him a scary story. But for some reason, it didn't help."

Batrick swung around, did a triple back flip, and landed between Fink and Fang.

"Scary stories are no help getting to sleep," he said. "I could've told you that. What you need is an adventure story to help you forget about being scared," he told Fink. "And I know the *perfect* one. Here goes . . ."

BATS AHOY!
AN ADVENTURE STORY

Once there was a brave pirate named Captain Batty, who sailed the seas with his loyal crew. Because Captain Batty was a little batty in the belfry, he gave his crew unusual orders all the time, like: "Swab the sails!" "Hoist the decks!" or "Walk the tank!"

His crew always did what he said, no matter how weird it was. Why? Because he was the boss.

One night, there was a terrible storm. Waves were crashing all around, and the captain and his crew nearly drowned.

"Batten the fishes!" Captain Batty shouted.

The crew wasn't sure what that meant, but they did it anyway. Unfortunately, it sank the ship.

The next morning, the crew woke up on a deserted island. Captain Batty found a bottle washed up on shore. There was something inside it.

Pop! He pulled out the cork. "Avast!" he said. Then he threw the bottle back in the sea.

"Um, I think there was something more in that bottle," said his first mate.

Captain Batty dipped the bottle out again and pulled a map from it this time. "Treasure *is* hidden on Bat Breath Island," he read. "X marks the spot."

"Yay! Hay! Hay! A treasure map! Let's go!" his crew said.

"Don't arrrrgue with me!" the captain shouted. "We're going to Bat Breath Island and that's final!"

"Um, this is Bat Breath Island," said his first mate.

"Avast!" said Captain Batty. "Let's go!"

But just then, a pirate ship full of growly owls dropped anchor. Captain Owly was the growliest of them all.

He grabbed the treasure map. "Thanks, Captain Batty!" He and his owl crew took off across the island to find the treasure.

"Come back, you scurvy navels!" shouted Captain Batty.

The owls looked confused.

"Um, I think he means 'scurvy knaves'," the first mate told them.

The owls hooted with laughter and kept going.

"After them, ladies!" Captain Batty ordered his crew.

Now the crew looked confused.

"I think he means 'mateys'," the first mate told them.

"Oh!" said the bat crew. So they all took off, chasing the owls over hills and under bridges and through trees.

But when they found the X, they were too late. The owl pirates were already digging. In no time, they found a shiny, golden treasure chest. Captain Owly opened it, looking excited.

When he saw what was inside, he scowled.
"Moths? Ick!"

Captain Batty's crew clapped. "Moths?
Yum! Hum! Hum!"

Captain Owly growled at the bats.
"I don't like moths. But I do like nice juicy. . .
BATS!"

"Rum for your lives!" said Captain Batty.
The bat crew just stood there.

"I think he means 'RUN'!!!" said the first
mate.

"Oh!" The bats took off. And the owls
chased after them.

But the bats were good at getaways. They did
loop-the-loops in the air. They did tuck-and-rolls
under logs. And they did corkscrews through
knotholes.

Around and around Bat Breath Island they all went. Over, under, through, and around. The owls were no match for the bats. They got dizzy and began to bump into each other.

While the owls were busy being dizzy, Captain Bat and his crew saw their chance and grabbed the treasure chest.

"Avast! We need a ship for all this looty!" Captain Batty jumped in the owls' ship.

"Um, I think he means . . ." began his first mate.

But his crew had already figured out what he meant and followed onto the ship. "Yo! Ho! Ho! Away we go!" they said.

"Come back, Captain Batty!" shouted Captain Owly as the bats sailed away.

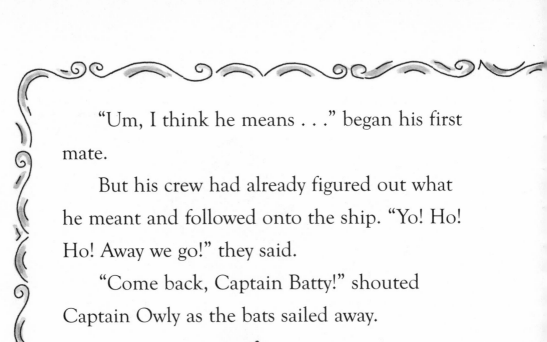

But Captain Batty just laughed. "That's 'Captain Booty' to you, Scuttlebutt!"

And with that, the bats sailed off into the sunset, munching on moth treasure.

THE END

"There. Are you sleepy now?" Batrick asked Fink.

Fink's eyes were big and round. They were wide open.

"Nope," he said. "Your adventure story was too exciting! Now I'll never get to sleep."

– 3 –

Kissy, Kissy

Just then, their sister Batsy flew out of her bed
in the hat stand. She whooshed her frilly scarf.
Sunlight glowed behind her like a spotlight.

"Why are you all still up, dahlings?" she asked.
"I've been batnapping since dawn."

"I can't sleep," said Fink.

"I told him a scary story, but it didn't help," said Fang.

"I told him an adventure story, but it didn't help either," said Batrick.

"Scary stories and adventure stories are no help getting to sleep," said Batsy. She folded her hands over her heart and sighed.

"What you need is a love story to make you feel all warm and marshmallowy inside," she told Fink. "And I know the perfect one. Here goes . . ."

CLEOBATRA: A LOVE STORY

Once upon a time, there was a beautiful princess who wore a long whooshy scarf. Her name was Cleobatra. Cleo for short.

Cleo was so beautiful that every prince in Batland wanted to marry her. Especially Prince Tutwinkle. He wrote a letter to Cleo every day that said: "Pleeze marrie me."

He couldn't spell, but he sure was dreamy. So Cleo decided to give him a chance to prove himself worthy.

"I might marry you if you make a bug catcher for me as a present," she told the prince.

"But I don't know how," he said.

Cleo gazed into the prince's dreamy eyes. "That's okay. I'll teach you how to make one," she said.

So they started weaving. It turned out that the prince was better at tangling than weaving, but soon they had made a net that was just right for catching bugs.

"Now will you marry me?" Prince Tutwinkle asked.

Cleo decided to give him a second chance. "Maybe. But only if you can catch a hundred bugs in ten minutes," she said.

"I've never caught any bugs before. My servants do that for me," said the prince.

"Hmm. Well, I'll show you how it's done," said Cleo, starting to frown. "Watch this."

She dipped and swooped. She dove and soared. In just ten minutes, she had caught a hundred bugs in her net.

"Now will you marry me?" asked Prince Tutwinkle.

Cleo decided to give him one last chance. "Not unless you fix enough buggy snacks to last me a whole week."

"But I can't cook," said the prince.

"Why am I not surprised?" asked Cleo, beginning to feel rather grumpy. "All right. I'll show you how. But this time you have to help."

Together they made beetle chips, cricket dip, and mosquito muffins. But the prince was better at snacking than helping.

"Now will you marry me?" Prince Tutwinkle asked when they'd finished.

Cleobatra thought about it for half a
second. She remembered that she had done
most of the work. Suddenly the prince didn't
seem quite so dreamy any more.

"No, thank you," she told him politely.

"Then can I have a muffin?" asked the prince.

"Okay, even though you didn't say 'pretty
please,'" said Cleo.

"How about a kiss?" asked the prince.

Cleo just sighed and bonked him on the head.

So Prince Tutwinkle went away and married somebody else.

And Cleobatra lived happily ever after.

🦇 **THE END** 🦇

"That's not a love story!" said Fink.

"It's a dumb story!" said Fang.

"A dumb girl story!" said Batrick.

"Well, that's the thanks I get for trying to help!" huffed Batsy, whooshing her scarf again.

"It was bad enough before," complained Fink. "But now I'll have to forget that kissing story if I ever want to get to sleep!"

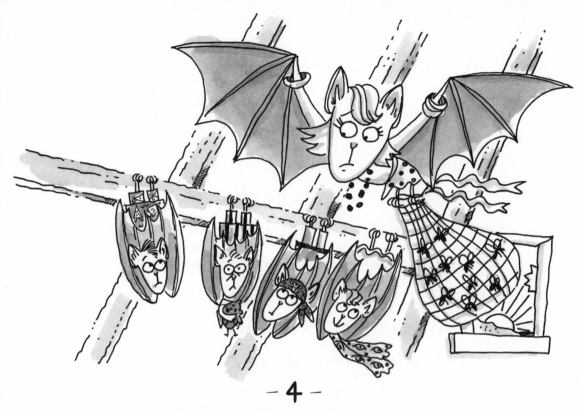

— 4 —
Nighty, Night

Just then, Mom Bat fluttered in through the window. "Sorry I'm late. I was catching mosquitoes for breakfast tomorrow. Why are you still awake?" she asked.

"Because Fink can't sleep," they all said at once.

"I told him a scary story," said Fang.

"I told him an adventure story," said Batrick.

"I told him a love story," said Batsy.

"But nothing helped," said Fink.

"Hmm. That's quite a problem. But I have an idea." Mom Bat went to the kitchen and hung the bag of mosquitoes she'd collected. Then she came back and gathered her bat children close.

"I love scary stories," she told Fang.

"And exciting ones," she told Batrick.

"And romantic ones," she told Batsy.

"But since it's bedtime, I think what you need
is a bedtime story," she told Fink. "And I know the
perfect one. Here goes . . ."

BATNAP:
A BEDTIME STORY

Once upon a time there were four bat children who were a family.

One moonlit night they had lots of fun together with their friends. They played hide-and-squeak among the twinkling stars and bat tag among sparkly fireflies. They played bowling-for-beetles on an old log, bobbing-for-bugs in an old pond, I-spy-a-spider-web in an old barn, and where's-worm-o? in an old apple orchard.

And last of all they had a nighttime picnic and ate doodlebug butter and June bug jelly sandwiches.

Then morning came. The sun peeked out and its warm, golden smile lit up the land, turning night into day.

And it whispered, "Bedtime for bats."

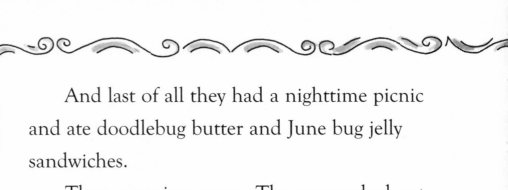

One by one, the bats began to yawn. They didn't want to stop playing, but they were so tired. So they said good day to their friends, knowing they'd see them again soon.

One by one, they flew home to their attic.

Mother Bat was there to welcome them. They told her about all the fun they'd had that night. She smiled and listened. Then she gave each bat child a hug and, one by one, they curled up to sleep in their nice, cool, shadowy attic.

Outside the window, the sun shone brightly. Inside, Mother Bat sang to the bat children as they snuggled in. Their wings fluttered and folded over their eyes.

Soon, they were all dreaming about the fun they would have the very next night when they woke up again.

And while they slept, Mother Bat watched over them and kept them safe.

"Nighty night, my children," she whispered.

THE END

"There—did that help?" Mom Bat asked softly.

But no one answered.

ABOUT THE AUTHOR
AND THE ILLUSTRATOR

JOAN HOLUB is a big dingbat who likes to hang around her office writing stories on her computer. She adores adventure stories, scary stories, and especially love stories, and she has published over one hundred and ten books for children. Everyone in her family is batty, and they all have pointy ears. She has many pets, including two fuzzy toy bats named Squeaky and Echo who hang from her ceiling. Joan writes mostly at night when she's alone in her cave. Around midnight, she brushes her fangs and goes to bed, where all her dreams are happy ones. Visit her at www.joanholub.com.

MERNIE GALLAGHER-COLE began drawing and painting at an early age and was influenced by her father, who worked as a graphic designer and watercolorist. She has known what she wanted to be since she was a child.

Mernie lives in West Chester, Pennsylvania, with her husband, two children, and a cat. Everybody in her house loves to draw . . . except the cat.